I HEAR YOU'RE RICH

I HEAR YOU'RE RICH

stories

DIANE WILLIAMS

SOHO

The following stories have appeared in *Harper's Magazine*: "One Woman and
Five Men," "I Fixed My Hair," "Can This Be I?" "Fling," and
"For Example, the Son."

The following stories have appeared in *London Review of Books*: "'Gladly!',"
"Seated Woman," "Tassel Rue," "To What Beautiful End?" "Riviera,"
"Mother of Nature," "Chuck," "Fredella," "Catalpa," "The Realist," and
"Zwhip-Zwhip."

These stories first appeared, sometimes in a slightly different form, in
BOMB: "Picturesque in the Extreme"; in *Conjunctions*: "Tale of Passion"; in
Granta: "Nancy's Victory"; in *INQUE*: "A Slew of Attractions"; in *N + 1*:
"Each Person to Her Paradise," "Take Your Dress Off," "The Assignment of
Fate"; in *The New Yorker*: "Live a Little"; in *Southwest Review*: "We Had a Lot
of Fun Dancing," "Tom's Fine."

Published by Soho Press, Inc.
227 W 17th Street, New York, NY 10011

Library of Congress Cataloging-in-Publication Data
Williams, Diane, author.
I hear you're rich : stories / Diane Williams.
Other titles: I hear you are rich
Description: New York, NY : Soho, [2023]
Subjects: LCGFT: Short stories.
Classification: LCC PS3573.I44846 I34 2023
DDC 813'.54—dc23/eng/20221024
LC record available at https://lccn.loc.gov/2022050303

ISBN 978-1-64129-478-2
eISBN 978-1-64129-479-9

Printed in the United States of America

10 9 8 7 6 5 4 3 2 1

To
Rebecca Godfrey

Yes, I know you pity me, and you want to take care of me and you'd like to be selfish in a way that you've never tried before—an unbending, melting way . . . —MAX BODENHEIM

I HEAR YOU'RE RICH

CONTENTS

———◆———

ORIEL?

———◆———

We were in the room where there is often a deep stream of daylight.

And my husband's mother had made sunshine cake for us, but since she did not like to walk—it hurt her legs—I was the one who carried the platter with the sumptuous cake to the table.

But where best to look as I went forward? At the cake? Or at their faces? This task takes common sense and balance as do all my others.

What to name our baby?—a sobriquet that means rich? Why not helper of humankind?—ardent or dawn? Deirdre, I like, but the name means sorrow—or Oriel?

So we ate cake and claimed happiness for the birth event that will come soon enough and the name I prefer for our daughter is Clara—which means shining and bright. And on our walk home I noted leaves much darker than others toward the center of a tree that I focused on.

The shape of the shadows? A scrap of a shadow maintained its roundness and then that shadow started to move and next I felt a sharp tapping on my back, caused by a stiff prod—by a wand of some sort, but when I turned to look, I saw no pointed object, and no one.

My husband, Stephen, said, "Jean, what's wrong?" He said, "Which is it?"

A girlish figure with her children and with their full voices in tow, casually passed us by, while spreading loving-kindness and grace, which I think may have become fashionable.

THE TUNE

———

Several birds had worms in their mouths, but one did not, and he whistled.

I whistled.

The whistling bird flew a bit beyond me and then settled again on the fence and I pursued him with the only tune I could manage until he answered back while he jumped to the ground at my feet.

He was my creature briefly. We didn't even vary the volume.

What I like best is taking my pleasure alongside somebody I barely know in such spasms.

START HERE

I got to the building that was a church that had a high ceiling and a long stair going down and a woman was coming after me, an elderly woman, but I didn't know her name. She was in a hurry. She said, "Tell the pastor that I saw you." I said okay, but I didn't remember who the pastor was or the woman's name. Why didn't I just tell the woman that? I just said okay to please her and it was dishonest.

And even though I was indoors, I thought, Let's see if I can fly, and I was floating around. People were looking at me and I said, "Don't try to do this! This takes a lot of practice."

I was happy and I was chubby. I had on some kind of woolen clothing.

I wonder what would have happened if I hadn't flown?

A SLEW OF ATTRACTIONS

———◆———

I was Diane Williams leaving town and I had left my family behind too, as well as a situation that had overwhelmed me.

My seatmate slept and we had an undemanding climb into the air, as the Airbus carried us above a slew of attractions.

And then we endured the severe stress of turbulence that lasted for too long, but the steward said he was not concerned and that the wings of the plane can bend quite easily to accommodate such trouble—and to show me how, he stretched his arms up high above his head.

The cabin was dim and then light entered at a low angle and further illumined the pages of my book.

My seatmate inquired about the book that tells a story much like my own. It is necessarily controlled and the personalities are abstracted. The novel is *Murder in Estoril* by Edith Templeton.

My seatmate said, "Life! This is the way to look at it!"

It was a cloud she pointed to that had flanking branches, fancy curly touches, and a generous nature that had to be the creation of a god who had forgotten how angry she is.

We heard for the trip's remainder the shifting of some invisible plane parts that made a low-grade cracking sound that I had to worry over.

On land, as in the air, I check the timepiece I wear often. Its second hand seems to tremble when it advances and its dial presents such a modern face.

My own face is old style. I have seen my face in a seventeenth-century painting, *A Girl and Her Duenna*.

The duenna is extremely amused and her eyes are my eyes, as is the tint of her skin and her forehead's contour.

She presses a kerchief against her mouth and chin and she will guffaw for ages—has done.

And do you know where I am this minute?—do you?

Where I am has an urban flavor and I ask myself to please make plain what my laughing matters are.

KEEPSAKE

I received a strong smooth cock that had nearly lifted itself out of itself—such a feat—but I could not keep it.

TO WHAT BEAUTIFUL END?

To what end does my husband customarily push his knee between my legs before he falls asleep, with his chest against my back?

But I think he was like a scrappy fox who barked while he ran away from me. He did that.

He was gone for about a month, but then he returned—and to what purpose?—and what do I want?

Doesn't everybody want to learn, to explore—and to interpret the actions of people, and then I like to add in what romance I can, and then play with what little I have learned for all that it is worth.

When Clement recently took me to Orio's, he told the waiter—"My daughter and I will have the chicken pie."

And I do love the pie, but why call me his *daughter*? Why?

We have tried out courtesy with one another for our safety's sake, but I have no choice but to report danger. To whom? To him.

"Who has the yellow hair?" I asked about the metallic loop that I found in the tub.

"It must have come down through the pipe from three C," is what he replied.

I took a hot bath last evening, lathered, scrubbed myself and when I got into bed, Clement entered me matter-of-factly after I had turned my back on him.

What happened next is that in the morning my hands were rightly in action, but not entirely guided, which is why the glass florist's vase next to the mixer fell and smashed into a whole batch of sad, but very sparkly charms that had jumped widely.

In some such similar cases, as when I drop a plate, there will only be a chink in the middle of it—or once I had a dish, with finely drawn flowers and leaves, crack neatly into four pretty, piece-of-pie slices that I trashed, but that at first I had to marvel at.

And I suppose that I am at my most promisingly *expressive* when I snap. Sometimes I snap.

But this time I got there only halfway, not the whole.

ZWHIP-ZWHIP

Her son is zigzagging on the lawn behind her house and he holds his new toy in his arms as if it is a babe in his arms.

It is the Easy Disk—which is painless to catch, cuts through the wind, floats on the water, flies up to one hundred and twenty feet, and is composed of a flexible, grippy material—but still, he has no one to play with.

His son is out there also, although his son is not yet old enough to walk, and is not interested in crawling either.

His son speeds along on his knees by swinging his arms and races away from his father, while his grandmother idles alone inside of her house on the headland.

The alcove the old woman sits in features objects that may impress her guests—except that through time she, herself, has been well humbled.

Her son enters the room to say, "*You are so rude to me!*"

"Yes, I am," she says. "Where is Neddie?

"Napping."

"Please leave me be," she says.

Then Neddie can be heard.

"It will be my turn to cry," she says, "when he stops crying."

How will that little boy fare?

"*Neddie, that is not for climbing!*" his grandmother calls—but the boy does nothing further to improve the old woman's mood. She does not feel appreciated and quite possibly she hates Neddie.

Blue jays in the pine tree let loose their unmusical jeer calls and in some other more ingratiating atmosphere elsewhere—say, where cardinals live—the locale is heavenly.

It could be that the Easy Disk's zeal in action sets a good example for boys and girls, as does Neddie's stacking toy.

This is a set of graduated color rings— the brilliant basics—for the child to grasp and to shake, and the plastic rings smack at one another, as the child puts them into their places.

His father takes up the game, too, beside his little boy, and this is the developing scene: The biggest ring has been situated wrongly at the top of the tower by the child, and so requires shifting.

"Will you just play, play, and dawdle?"— the mother asks her son. "*Is this what you intend to do with the rest of your life?*"

"How funny you are," says her son. "I don't know if I ought to."

. . .

Dinner is over and his mother delays her retreat from it in order to first fully open and smooth out her linen napkin on the tabletop. She then succeeds in producing a folding feat of middling difficulty, a pyramid.

She prevails as a large body, slow walking, taking short strides from the table, thinking, *Is it too much to ask for?—that the happiest, proudest day of my life will arrive?—when it is all I have ever aimed for.*

The summer night still reflects light—and when the child Neddie is put to bed, the old woman's son sets about navigating his soccer ball, with his toes, or the whole sole of his foot, on the promontory, gently.

"GLADLY!"

———◆———

He is a figure I once engaged with for years, amid scenes with nearly religious significance attached to them.

And by chance, this Saturday, I had witnessed him stepping away from a park path and stooping beneath the leaf cover—only to put his hand against the tree trunk.

He smiled when he saw me, but when I

reached him he was speechless and sour, and then he proceeded on his way headlong.

If only he had said, "You come with me."

I fell back, stood at a distance.

But let us leave a famous man for a moment.

Two objects, that had been abandoned, surely through some fault of their own, showed up in the border grass.

And detritus is common around here, but these two items were an arousing color and brand-new enough to engage my interest. The clean canvas All Star high tops were perhaps my size.

And, then, as if this footwear could somehow stay the same while it changed—the shoes showed up as ruined goods. One of the pair had a long rip at the heel.

Well, where I was, is where I often go for the sights, for a walk at day's end—for deep breaths, or just to listen to the faint clicking— for how my own feet smack at the path.

A boy of five or six was picking up handfuls of nuts that I thought were meant for the squirrels. He was inspecting the ground and most efficiently scavenging, stuffing his pockets, and repeatedly patting his large, jammed pockets.

He'll be known in later life for his gluttony or for his enterprise.

What am I—I wonder, dear god—now best known for?

WE HAD A LOT OF
FUN DANCING

———◆———

The normal precautions and rules were somewhat out the window. I made my costume and had some sort of shoes I could dance in. Her costume was something with feathers—something birdlike.

You could buy beer or wine and the people that you came with soon disappeared.

I found myself with her and around other people I didn't know and she had about her, I thought, an aura of world-daring, except that I was not ready—that was for sure.

She gave me compliments and smiles and we had a lot of fun dancing.

She was quite a bit older, I guessed, so when she said she lived nearby, sex was on my mind.

We ended up in bed and after hugging and kissing for a while, we proceeded to the more essential part, having intercourse.

I had little experience. Eventually, I landed in the right space and then after, it wasn't a long time, she pulled back. So at that point I was looking at her.

I didn't have preservatives—whatever they're called, starts with a *p*. She said she had protection and she said, "Let's complete it." And I did reach a climax. I don't know if she did. I just felt awful.

She was talking about continuing our relation and I said, yes, yes. I felt exhilaration and shame, shame because I did not see a future with Margareta. I was not a good candidate and I did not want to give her any hope. We spoke on the phone and I was very sad.

So, do I even know why I submitted to her continued pursuit—in the end?

Ever since and years later, I have stayed on with Margareta, all the while considering myself unalterably naïve.

For instance—what is it that constitutes deep and enduring affection? This remains to be seen.

And I am still bent on strictly assessing myself.

Is my background well-rounded enough? Have I got a passably pleasant personality?—the right combination of theoretical and practical knowledge to remain reasonably competent, acceptably up to the standard in everything that I do?

Or, can I make it look like that?

Am I qualified for my reward?

SEATED WOMAN

O h, I had my worm's eye view of him when I was down on the carpet to pick up my ink pen that had slipped off of my lap when I stood. I saw the canopy of his jaw, his jawbones.

God . . . will I never know if I make things better for Victor?

I would need to go along with him and there was no denying he was piqued, and I was putting up resistance. He wanted to show me something.

But beyond Victor, I looked toward curtain folds—or elsewhere to where this room flows into another and then back out the window toward a swath of bleached blue sky where I saw an airplane that seemed to be going far too slowly—walking specd! Why didn't it fall out of the sky!

I followed behind Victor as I carried my mug of tea—mindful not to pour or to spatter, and then he halted and pointed. And to begin with, I looked at his mouth too full of teeth and open.

But when I took in what he saw—it was terribly embarrassing.

Well, the atmosphere here is thick with dismissal and with so much I have done and do wrong.

I drew tight the knot in the belt of my robe. It was the best I could think to do. But I guess the noose now was around my waist.

A paper wasp was making headway on the sill. It was accelerating with rightwardness, and I should have said *bravo* to it—because the thing had been nearly unopposed—up until this moment.

FOR EXAMPLE, THE SON

———◆———

What are they going to do now, folks? The most necessary step?

The father had a grip on the boy's wrist near the lilac bush, which the mother sat beside and the mother said, "There isn't time for that, you know, now. I have to go get my tooth implant."

The boy sprang loose from his father and

31

then up an incline and the father ran after and held on, as the child plunged about.

Don't spit on your mother! Never spit on her. You have to say you are sorry to your mother!

The boy strongly has a sense he should be elsewhere, whereas the mother likes to believe she is a practical young woman and she is by all appearances placid. The father thinks himself mighty in battle.

And that boy, Derek Hood, is now a man. Born in Fredericksburg, Virginia, he still lives there. Hood is both distinguished and cruel and has exerted himself to relieve poverty and sickness.

One stormy evening his young son says, "It's raining!" The boy's mother says, "No, it's not."

"But," the boy insists, "I hear the *di di di di di di di di!*"

"I don't hear it either," his father says.

He never found anyone as difficult to hit as that little boy.

LIVE A LITTLE

———◆———

His wife, Ariadne, rinses egg dregs from yet another dish, but the sticky residue chooses to stick to her fingers!—and she may be a touch dismayed by the sensation.

Her husband has to frown because he notices his wife frown and because all the members of his family, it seems to him, are acting sad or are actually sad.

But the back door of the house has been

opening and shutting often—and for the husband, the father—that sound hints at his idea of a happy summertime. That is the significance of that sound for him.

He is at that door as he follows his wife, Ariadne, to where she is stretched out on a garden chaise longue, and a child or two of theirs is out there also in the sandbox.

But these days, his getting too close to Ariadne might result in a variety of symptoms for either one of them, ranging from moderate to severe to fatal—he must realize.

He puts his hands on Ariadne's throat when she speaks to him, pinching it just enough to snap a stem, say, but not enough to kill a whole plant.

Then he returns to the house to escape her, but she finds him rather quickly to exhibit her spilling eyes and her tightened mouth.

But don't ardor and rage amount to— usually appear—nearly the same? For the husband, at any rate, they do.

And when he takes into account their children—he thinks that perhaps they are not so sad, for what do they lack?

Today the family's sandbox is abundantly

moist, wet enough for the children to be busy making cakes and digging gritty holes.

It is for the best that the twins enjoy stabbing at the sand. They are strengthening their finger and hand muscles with their toy shovels and they absolutely relish listening to the grains of sand hiss.

The natural enthusiasm of this sand is so influential, so persuasive as it is poked and sprayed and even knuckled under—or just played with a bit.

TALE OF PASSION

They latched their mouths together, paus-
ing only to permit themselves some rest
at regular intervals—and they did these cal-
isthenics in the Beatrice Pebble Garden for
well over an hour, while in twisting poses.

Well, I have never done that, but perhaps I should have, because I know this man,
where he lives, the putty-colored walls. I *really*
know—his pots, plates, food, the nice places

to sit and to lie down—the richly happy, pro-
fusely thriving, and glowing appetites he is
capable of, and also we have similar laughs.

Dragonflies, in the garden that day, of
many varieties and sizes were crisscrossing—
and they seemed especially hysterical.

And this man appeared a changed man,
in somewhat sketchy form from where I sat,
because he has trimmed his hair and he has
altered his usual garb.

A tree, cut to a stump, is behind the woman,
from which slim branches have grown upward
and they are arcing and flowering again.

So, who left the garden first? I did.

In years past, I tried to find what I needed
from this man, even sweetness, and whenever
I was able, I tried to take it from him.

There was a park where I grew up with long
rows of chestnut trees, which in the spring-
time bore towers of flower clusters. There
were swings for children. There was a foun-
tain that shot water into the sky and there
were women—we'd call them park ladies.
They handed out large building blocks and

chess games, and there was a sandpit, small shovels and buckets, and sand forms with which you could make cookies.

And I tell myself that this park is still functioning today—where it is not necessary for either the adults, or for the children, to strive too wildly.

FREDELLA

——◆——

One woman grew her hair so long it dragged across the floor as she walked. People thought she was pleasing to look at and she wore highly decorated clothing.

And facing the gods was joyful for her too. Foremost, she had to face herself—and she thought she was so inspirational.

She did not see her darker purposes . . . These lay far away in veiled areas.

Invariably she says to her husband, You are right!—and very often he says, True.

Such is their mode, their temperate manner.

Naturally there are those exigencies, calamities that underpin everyday life. How does the couple keep going with gusto?—also sometimes the woman can't walk at all.

Now, I wouldn't have thought so—but she developed severe arthritis in the talo-navicular joint, one of the many small joints in the ankle.

But it is not possible to worry ourselves over the concerns of every little animal that has to take care of itself.

Let us enter their house to see the orange folding chairs that are punchy and the radiators that have been painted to match.

An armchair has been placed by the window where the woman prefers to spend her holidays.

By the way, she plays the tuba. When she was a young woman she dedicated herself to the tuba. The tuba is capable of everything. People are just figuring that out. And if you don't like the sound of it, you can't blame everything on the player or on the instrument—some of the problem is in the music.

I HEAR YOU'RE RICH

———◆———

"I am afraid I've overdone it," Connie said, and she patted her belly, and from the street I heard a hammer that was hitting metal somewhere.

I was eating their fish and little cakes that had cheese in them, and vegetables that can stink up one's breath after they are eaten—endives and radishes. And I was fortunate to know them—Constance and George Mock.

"Can you give me some of your money? I hear you're rich," I said because of the wine.

Connie said, "Rosie!"

"Let's call that a joke," George said. "That was a joke."

I was mortified—also tearful because they had decided to leave town.

I am too old for this—but I am still unmistakably in need of parents, and the Mocks know it. They also know that their sad daughter Stephanie has always called me her best friend.

"Can you get us coffee, George?" Connie said.

I could see Mr. Mock in the kitchen, stepping across their checkerboard floor, onto the black squares only, diagonally, so then I jumped up and I hopscotched in to help him.

The Mocks kindly took me along to their island house where Connie gifted me a charm—a carved limestone bird whose smile, I think, looks like a smirk.

"I hope you will wear it," she said. "I hope you will love it."

Arnold Turner, their neighbor, came by and he tugged at my arm and he said, "Did you mean *her* for me?"

"Arnold, look what we did!" George said, pointing toward their flowing grasses, the tropical flowers.

"I prefer the woods!" Mr. Turner said. "My daughter has the woods! My son has the sea! What do *you* have?" he asked me. "I expect you have a career?"

"Yes, I do," I answered.

He had no further questions. His lips were shut, hands clasped, but his chin is dimpled just like my brother's is.

So Mr. Turner did not have to wait days before we were alone in the throes and he was sweating and puffing in my company.

What a relief. Peace at last. I am highly sexed.

Many persons in the past have also given me their all—Dylan, Andy, Chris, Matt, Connor and Bill Kawa, and Judd Friedenberg.

Food was forever being served at the Mocks' and when I woke, I could just grab for something to eat—as if the biscuits and breads were dangling from branches.

My breakfast was ample enough to last the whole day and then I'd head for their pool where the luncheon buffet was spread out at one end.

Yes, I swim. I think it is the closest thing to walking on air, although it is strenuous.

I lie down and I face the world there.

TAKE YOUR DRESS OFF

———◆———

"Take your dress off," he said. "Leave your underwear on."

And she must have known that when most people see her they think, *You are so alluring.*

He also thought that she was strong, physically strong, although, when he said to her, "You must be strong," she said, "No!"

"Did you ever think you'd be standing here like this?" he said.

He looked out the window while he unknotted his tie and he saw simplified forms outlined with dark contours, everyday three-dimensional forms.

What did she see?—the sash and the sill and his hands on his own person.

Would there be pent-up forces at play or "rides" when they got into bed?

Yes.

Of course, there's the anticipated stretch of his crucial part at the start that creates the strengthening effect, that gives him leave to reach out beyond his defensive wall. He is so fucking lucky and he has wherewithal.

There had been many directives from him to her to do this and to do that.

But let me tell you something about all of her rooms! These rooms have been touched by the vanguard modern.

Her home is like a small kingdom-come where there are hard surfaces to take comfort in—a white metal-and-glass table, a red side chair the color of Heinz Tomato Soup.

Similar effects, for her, were created by the fact that Geoffrey Sklamberg was busy screwing her.

Also there are the carved-in-stone, bell drop swags, along with the repeating, tied ribbons that she always sees—that are featured on the building façade across the street, but these for some reason make her feel sick to look at.

She once came across a limestone frieze of a grazing beast on a leash beside a blossom that was as big as a tree—and for an instant the sight gladdened her.

Mr. Sklamberg and Veronica Nash disentangled themselves and broke abruptly with a sharp twist into two buff parts.

Stare at them! Should they be further adorned or engorged?

Veronica went off to use the toilet. She was conscious of pain or an ache, the need to urinate.

She did not want Sklamberg to hear her splashes or any other evacuations.

She extended her stay in the sheltered hollow of the bathroom for as long as she was able.

Well, the weather was relieving. Yes, it was

the tenderest, the plumpest—dripping, and packed tightly.

Veronica heard herself speaking when she returned to the bed and she thought she was brave.

So let her say something! Let her speak!

She might embarrass us.

CATALPA

———◆———

"Did you ever find out about that tree?" the wife asks.

"A lady in the park told me—it's *catalpa!*"

"A lady in the park? Who is the lady in the park?"

"She probably had a dog," her husband says.

"*You were flirting with a woman in the park! Is she beautiful?*"

Losing his balance as he goes, owing to a crack in the pavers—her husband leaves her side.

The once well-anchored man falls down and this becomes one of those village-life scenes that features a recumbent figure, who is an object of interest to others.

The husband lies there for a spell on his belly—face forward and chin up—before he stands. And his wife finds a place to sit beside a garden that achieves a planted-by-nature effect.

How lovely!—a passerby thinks while looking at the wife.

She puts him in mind of the feminine ideal, a bit too pretty, as she looks sideways and smiles, frowns, glances upward.

An aquatic garden is close at hand, woodland trails, and an information booth. The City of New York owns these grounds.

And the husband—he is also a resource in great demand, thought by many women to be strong and protective.

His wife stamps her foot near the paw of a squirrel. "He is too near!" she says to her husband, who is now at her elbow.

"He is eating," her husband says, "a banana chili."

"What is a banana chili? Oh, from somebody's lunch. *He is following us!*"

Other animals have followed her, of course. Slow dogs.

Once she followed a strolling pigeon for more than several blocks and wondered, Why does this pigeon choose to walk? Why not just fly?

She is not in a hurry either—to face the facts of her marriage.

She never knew a pigeon walked distances.

I will not disturb this bird!—she was thinking, even though it could not care less about her.

How far will it—she was guessing—can it go on this way?

THE ASSIGNMENT OF FATE

———◆———

Someone glorious had built this temple or call it a house that we had bought tickets to swing through.

Nevertheless, one of the first things I like to do is to take stock of the gift shop, an enduring practice. It seems entirely natural to go to the gift shop first, because it eases the necessary transition into the spectacular.

I examined a platter depicting a humorous and lively fish and a terra-cotta pot. I was scorning so much else.

You know, terra-cotta is very widespread. It is used by every civilization.

I selected note cards that feature images of women bearing up. These are caryatids.

One of these women is particularly sensual in her pose, yet her expression is modest. Another's face is decidedly masculine. Her chin projects nearly as far forward as her nose and she stares aggressively ahead. Yet most are downcast, not revealing trapped sexual energy, not revealing energy.

My own head started aching and shortly we joined up with a guide who told us that dinner on these premises was followed by a formal dance held in the drawing room. Music was furnished by an orchestra from New York City. The centerpiece on the dining table might have been a yachting trophy and there were once sixty servants on the estate!

Dominic said, "This is funny." And I said, "Why?"

Our safety, we were told, was the primary concern and we were told to be careful going up and down the stairs and that we should regard ourselves as if we personally lived here.

Everything is aristocratic and stylish and I could barely recall our hasty morning departure from Little Neck—from bitterness, political stresses, and from our immoral conduct. That was all blurred and misshapen.

However, this Vanderbilt mansion, I recall it well. When it was built it cost $660,000. Guests included nobility and an American president. And Louise Vanderbilt's bedroom carpet weighs over 2,300 pounds!

We heard that she was particularly contented when she did some of the things she did. She helped people in the community!—if there was illness, if there was poverty!

I saw a photographic portrait of her in which she appeared with her waist fashionably corseted painfully, no forced smile, jewelry on, a plumed fan in her hand, seemingly for my benefit, because I admire the fan so much.

I can imagine the fan bringing my life freshly to life as she points the fan all fluffy and blooming forward toward me—as if there are only clouds and space all around us and a blue ceiling.

I also have a fan, a hand-painted, Chinese fan made of paper and bamboo that shows off a mountain region landscape that includes a modern dam installation.

I don't use the fan nearly enough in summertime when I need it. The relic has been in the dark and unremembered. I don't use it. I never used it. Nobody ever used it. I wouldn't think of using it. I bought it. I just found it. I went looking for it.

When I close the fan, the fan sounds like an oaf who is burping or she is slurping soup, but when I open the fan!—I hear genteel and soft mechanical ticking.

FLING

———◆———

This is snug enough and the warm day allows for sitting outside, and she holds a flower stalk, a featherbell, and has tried forever not to be an ass, tried.

What about him? He's got a slip of paper in his hand while birds go by demonstrating all manner of flying styles—provoking, sweeping wings, or agitated.

"That goose is in pain too!" the old

woman says. "It must hurt it to fly like that and it sounds as if it's sick. It's hoarse!"

The old man's limbs don't hurt that much. Hers hurt. Her left foot, both knees. It's the heel of her left foot. Her left hand is at issue, naturally, under these circumstances, yes, and typically.

And it is not to her advantage that she often sleeps with her hands held up above her head, positioned as if for the Highland Fling.

The panicle on her lap—it's finished—has flattened.

And the elderly man and woman will yield to a superior force too—but in a good way?—sometime soon.

For now, they budge a bit—and the woman thinks, I am going to go inside and set the oven at four hundred and fifty and start the carrots.

The sparrow near the bent toe of her shoe takes off toward a tree as she rises from her lawn chair, and she wonders aloud, "How does he know I can't chase up there after him?"

And the old man?—he has had a wise idea too—which for him provides an intermission of sorts, and so . . . but as it happens he is napping when a small boy approaches and causes the woman to feel childish fear. "*What did you say?*" she asks the child.

"*I want to show you something!*" the little boy keeps saying. "*I want to show you show you something!*" and the boy is supposed to turn up in the nick of time and be much more intelligible, but this old woman just can't make him out.

In the meantime, we can look around at where they all are, where centuries ago, executions and floggings took place.

But this is also where this mister and the missus once stood and danced together—*walk, walk, walk, and step hold*—and there are the starry, late-blooming flowers, and the shadblow and a birch, and a shrubbery garden border.

The little boy has unknown ambitions and has just departed and the old woman cranks her head sideways, skyward.

And she doesn't wonder to what or to whom she says—*Bring down a big owl* or *Let me see a hawk down here so I can scare the hell out of him too!*

And this is almost the whole story I wanted to tell you—how an old wife left the shore—but she doesn't die yet, a minute or so after midday, just after saying, "I'll go in now . . ."

She lingers—although she hardly lingers at all. She is interested to see if she will make a spectacle of herself, or if she can possibly be very smart about it, or better yet—dainty.

TASSEL RUE

———◆———

The bird's voice was such a thick voice—
it could never have been carried away by
the high wind. It was a passionate voice that
might have answered the question, "What am
I living for?"—had there only been words to
accompany it.

And I did get to see the bird out on
a limb, opening and closing its mouth, its
breast pulsing.

Ruby had said, *There is the bird that is singing!*

Perhaps we had gotten this far flung once before, where we found the beautiful tassel rue that has such an ugly common name—false bugbane—together with large and sharp, saw-toothed leaves.

"See the bird!" Ruby cried again, and I said, "That's maybe a robin—" or a robin gone wrong. It had a robin's shape, but the coloring was off—speckled earth tones.

It stayed nearby—turned out it was a wood thrush. It flew away and then it returned to stand exactly in the same place.

"Is it lost?" Ruby asked. "Can a bird get lost?"

It stood. It stood, but, of course, it was disinclined to lie down endlessly at our side, like a dog.

If only I could have said often with clear conscience, "I'll go—then I'll be right back for just a minute and then you will never see me again—" Something like that, on so many occasions, to some women . . .

A young man in a cap swung around with his back to us when he came into the clearing.

He lunged forward, then drew in the bent leg, lunged again, and then departed. He might have been very handsome.

"You can tell, I think," Ruby said, "by how somebody moves that he is a good person. That man, I can tell, is a good person. He is not combative."

I thought, no, he's as sorry a sight as a gnat, as I picked a flower, then picked the flower apart. Some flowering plants provide an inspiration to do what?—to be elegant—suave?

I tell myself I am a prominent supporter of Ruby's and well familiar with her tendency toward idealizing. I am actively involved with that sort of thinking too, but not just in dreams. I have been pleading that we stay on together.

"Do you remember," I asked her, "what we agreed?"

"What we agreed?"

A complication. She bent her head lower and lower and at close range, in her curly hair, I saw the number six, the letter *C,* and a fishhook.

Hadn't she just been spirited and was she now distraught?—and I felt love for her.

And on this Sunday afternoon we were

supposed to be recompensed for the week of work, but apparently I had upset her.

My purpose is to hold Ruby or to catch or contain or to tame her.

I watched sparrows eating, tearing into dandelion buds. A robin was beating his head into the ground and Ruby kept on with, "See that!" and "See that!" and "What is that?"

We were hearing a series of shouts from a group of grackles and the area was piled high with the language of birds.

Emerging from the mouth of one of them was a hard passage I wished I could call my own. It had a hammering rhythm and made bold, heroic strokes.

I have a terrible tendency toward jealousy.

What else?

I intend to be unreservedly triumphant in love—that sounds good—also undefeated in all of the other drastically risky aspects of my life.

CHUCK

———◆———

But this story is not about Chuck. Chuck Chuck, so to say.

She cannot have endured the man for long, but she did—because hers is a tale of passion.

See how she smoothed her salvage—as she dusted the elk family figurines that Chuck gave her—as she tried to bring back strong memories of adoration or lust.

And can you believe that?—that Chuck Rosso, whom she had depended upon, refused to help her in the shower when she broke her leg. He never ever even offered to make her a cup of coffee!

So what does *this* mean? Was this a suicide?

She saw a dove dive headfirst off the parapet with its feet heaved up into the air.

And what about her own mental distress? She made no effort to minimize it while she viewed in a hand mirror the incline from her nose to her mouth, the whole world that was visible down to her chin.

Then she looked up and climbed higher to just the under part of a blue eye—for well she knows how unsafe it is to look herself in the eye.

Still and all she is a young woman with a soft shallow voice who came up with a plan in the midst of this. And that's Gwen Hay for you.

On that day she went to the market to stock up on things and she also needed money.

She shouldered the bank door, as she exited, with less force than she had used for her entry and the door yielded so slowly.

In addition, by dint of this act, she slightly injured her shoulder.

Yet she had pulled hard with her hands at the bank's weighted door to get inside and the next day, on a whim, she pressed and rubbed upward and downward on Garry Gibney's upper leg—did that, so that Garry asked Gwen if he could lie down on top of her and he received her consent, but she did not find him to be that stimulating or helpful.

As far as her romantic attachments, she almost always decides wrongly. Much of Gwen's appeal to men stems from her good qualities, which she is unable to showcase for drawn-out periods.

The problem is she has largely avoided full development—that is, a necessary extension of her personality.

She does know that good posture is always preferable to bad posture—except that it is hard to come by—and that one needs deeper inhalation ahead of exhalation.

A great deal of life is spent standing. The rib cage expands. She should be *really* perpendicular!

And she does love a long hike—along roadsides, over slopes, through disturbed areas.

But this is not a story about roaming or aimlessness.

When she walks around she does not drag herself forward and the strained, tightened zones behind her knees seem then to breathe easier.

Her gentle locomotion promotes a sense of extreme security and serenity.

And it is as if her knees are the ones to have fallen in love with her!

ONE WOMAN AND FIVE MEN

———◆———

She has said, "I don't make friends easily with men. I don't really like the trouble of them. I like the idea of men."

And yet, she has developed two effective modes of operating: survey the other's body, then stealthily approach, or lie still at first.

And her life has been one crowded calendar.

But look what we have here—nobody in a bed and instead a ramble in progress, as Mr.

Rollo Ryder conducts the woman on a moderate climb. And at the zenith—they both felt weaker, as if they had received a rough physical blow.

No!—not on account of their light physical exertions.

What caused the offense? It was the severe sight, as they looked out from the cliff, of rock formations with minimal vegetation.

And the wallop, of course, was nothing personal, was well-meant and all that.

And this incident has unreasonably increased the woman's dislike for Mr. Ryder, even though once, in his company, she did feel thoroughly and delightfully stretched.

But from where they stood that day, apparently, the bright light revealed pockmarks in the rock, the face of which was bony, freckled, pallid.

But supposing nothing more happens and that this is how the story sullenly ends.

So unfair—because just to the north lies a mountain range where—as it is told in *another* tale about this woman—she gets to keep company with a mountain god in the form of a dog—who possesses patience, intelligence, and gentleness.

EACH PERSON TO
HER PARADISE

———◆———

In the long run, as a sequel to our other less strenuous raptures, he undressed and put himself on the bed belly down—lying crossways across it.

This was his *come hither*. His arms were pressed against his sides, I think.

He was facedown, I think. Facedown, really? Like a swimmer. Were his arms really stretched out in front?

And the stress that ensued was not the strange thing.

I did my best, keeping my lower part centered when I met up with him—after he had moved his location and changed his posture accordingly.

I was awkwardly raising a leg, flexing a knee.

But this is my motto. *While you can't figure out how, you do it.*

And I was wearing my skin unfresh and sallow and some sympathetic restoration in that regard is still called for.

But by the time he stuck his hand out toward me . . . Did he then?

So . . . no, neither of us accomplished anything particularly tender then or later.

He had a habit—how he took my arm, as if with a heavy pincers, on a subway platform to maneuver us if we were in a crowd—and I really enjoyed that aspect of our relation.

Each person to her paradise.

That grip of his, as a matter of fact, was, and still is, when I think of it, a source of inspiration—like a legend or wisdom—like humor can be.

When water gushed down his body when he rose from the tub, after he had bathed, that flow of water was a drumroll.

The god in this story is this man and I do not accuse him of anything. I could.

MOTHER OF NATURE

My brother's words when I hear them these days seem not to go into my ears—but down some other deeper artery.

He said, "It's Mother's house and I just think of it as home."

"I would *never ever* go there today," I said. And we were in the middle of a paved two-way drive in the park, having left it up to the pack of people we were in among to decide whether it was prudent for us to cross.

The house that we grew up in—the great benefit of that house is that the finish and the presentation of its furnishings are like a shield that we might hold over our privates and the credit for this goes to our deceased mother.

The draperies are brocade—turned inside out—Mother said, in order to obtain a richer, faded effect—and everywhere in the world, and here, too, flowers have been enlisted to exude confidence.

In the foyer there's the carpet with carnations and an apple blossom wall covering. This house is a fitting setting for those who are able to enjoy unrelenting family life. A class of us fail. I did.

"I am never going there and I am never walking Jumbo again!" I told my brother, "*Ever!* He broke my wrist. I am never going to walk that dog again ever!" My father's dog.

Another father—this one was young—was swiftly conducting his hatted little girl in a stroller, but I overheard him say, "*What*, baby? *Why* do you think you stopped taking your naps?"

"Dad should get rid of it!" my brother said. "He dislocated my shoulder!"

At one time Jumbo's options had been to become lethargic, average, solid, plodding, very appealing, a winner all around, or unloved.

I have become bitter I fear.

Silence followed and then my brother gave me a rundown on his physio treatments, as opposed to the usual advice I hear from him—how to heal an unhappy marriage, how to break a bad habit. But for all that, I still asked why did he have to go back home.

Dad is so mean. There shouldn't be a reason.

Could there be a speck of my original self anywhere?—that I have left behind. God, and if I have forgotten about it, can it save me?

CAN THIS BE I?

Actually, I had walked into the hallway and disappeared into the bedroom briefly. Several of them danced and I heard Vida say about me, "He disappeared into the backyard."

She, Vida—once went everywhere with me, in the air, on foot, by car and train and still I can't now really claim her as a true friend. So, Vida was once my hope that everything in my life that was bad or sad would end.

Today I had set out deluxe vegetables—the spinach ring that Les loves, alongside a big cheese-egg float. And I enjoy washing the greens clear of their colonies of organisms, scanning the wrinkles and the cracks for their impurities over and over again.

Ted prodded the dessert, said he was tired, and griped about my squash that was too spicy.

"I'll tell you what let's do," I said.

Then Polly arrived angry. "Are there two Gulfs by any chance? You said to go five blocks beyond the station!"

I forgot about Ted. I was glad of Alice's presence. I adore Alice and I hooked my hand around her elbow.

I guess I expect too much goodwill, especially from Alice, deference and enamoredness. There it is!—what I want from Alice, who had just found a framed photograph of my father.

"I liked him, but he didn't like me," I said. "Do I look like him around the eyes? I don't have the pointed chin."

But Alice cold-shouldered my father in order to put a cheese cone on her plate and then other people followed her around and I know she causes sexual excitement.

Oh, eat, drink, and explore. I love those ideas.

My thought was—if I left the house now, I could return to my party at six.

I did. I took a walk around the block—got a cheap cocktail—where I could also get a quick bite in a shushed atmosphere.

But what if I could have gone anywhere?

I would go to Japan probably. I'd like to go into one of those Japanese temples or estates to get a feeling of the emptiness of the rooms. Why emptiness?

I am saying *empty*—why do I say *empty*?—because of how I grew up inside of clutter.

Very often a room is a rectangular space—corners and juts. When getting into a room like that with all that clutter—the shape of the room just falls away.

So I wonder if I'd feel any better in an empty room—if the room has a strong presence . . . yet it is cordial.

EVERYTHING IS WONDER

———————

These fruits produce ruddy light—are sound and smooth and tiny-sized and the woman thinks it is so thoughtful how they offer themselves up as a treat, as if they could, to a prosperous individual such as herself.

On the other hand, her soup will spit on people and so it sits atop a paper towel.

Her husband had said, "No, not like that! First put this under it—" because the broth can spatter or slop when its lid is opened or shut.

The woman nearly kissed the little fruits before she ate them, but then she was choking on one of them while her husband never bothered to go to her side—even though she still has her youthful slenderness, her teeth and her hair, for all the good that'll do her.

Nevertheless, she likes to cuddle her husband and to dote on him. And after unaided, she had quieted, he said, "How about that soup? I'm hungry."

Why doesn't he ask her for the dessert that looks like pie and tastes like cake that's next to the soup on the fridge shelf. It's as beautiful as a daffodil and this is a really good pastry, well-behaved and dotted with cherries, and it has a tender texture.

There is an astonishing collection of edible wealth here and, in addition, the woman wears carved black onyx and gold earrings that are worth one thousand dollars.

It is sad to ask, please don't ask—but what is the measure of this wife's utility, character, desirability?

Why did I ask?

RIVIERA

So what about the mother and daughter's shared jealousy, guilt, strain, or pain—those?

Oh, must everybody have to deal with those?

Don't imagine.

The mother is a slightly brave, a slightly unembarrassed person who can be quite social and today she has just written this letter.

Dear Teresa,

Well, I don't know how to say I am wretched. It is terribly sad that I am living at the end of the saga. Sorry that you are too. Do you have another point of view you can share?

Ann is here. Are you coming?

Frances

"Hello! Hello!" It is Joe Lesko at the door and he has brought cucumbers for Frances Reff and for her daughter.

"And some tarragon. It's great in omelets. Finally," he says, "something for you from my garden. It will be interesting to see where all this is headed."

"Liverwurst is my favorite," Mrs. Reff says, "that's what I like," while her daughter Ann notes for the first time that Lesko looks just like Benjamin Franklin—a person who is curious, but not curious about her.

"Did Daddy live here, Ann?"

"*Mother, he built this house!*"

There is a better way for talking to people—Mr. Lesko is thinking—than my way or theirs, as he drives home on a public road made up of complicated swirls that lead to his cottage on the lake.

The room where he receives guests is unlike the rest of his house and many unhappy times are spent in this front room, which is spare and bare, although a vase of thistles and wildflowers and a folded newspaper help to make it look as if somebody lives in it.

His recent crop of creamy-skinned Boothby's Blondes are in a bowl on the kitchen counter and he is so pleased that as promised, they have no bitter aftertaste. He hadn't cared for the sourness of the lemon cucumbers he tried out last year. Next year he'll try the Poona Kheera, said to be tender, crisp, and delicious—that can be eaten skin and all, or perhaps the Painted Serpent, which is not really a cucumber. It's a melon, heavily ribbed.

Lesko hears a tiny sneeze from the front path through an open window.

To accommodate Ann Reff, he offers her fresh coffee, warm food.

"I couldn't stand it anymore," she is saying. "There is such unjust treatment. I had pulled a carrot out of the ground and dusted it off and I ate it and I was told I couldn't do that! Do you know when I was a girl my toys were put out in the yard in an open bin for any other children to help themselves! *Oh, Joe! I love you so much! I've loved you so much! I worship you! I've loved you so much!*"

"No," Lesko says. "You are mistaken."

Not that he minds the outburst and the general unease he is feeling that he is so used to.

And to Ann he says, "*Come here!*" even though he has never described her to himself down to the smallest detail, nor will he ever.

PICTURESQUE
IN THE EXTREME

———◆———

What could be better?—I remember thinking.

I'd be encountering a most popular person of vital interest to all of us who love or who handle women.

And beautiful nudes have a long, long history with me—and it was reasonable to expect that I'd be successful.

Well, I knew her face well. Her eyes, nose, and mouth are standard size and simplified. Unclothed, the whole of her is smoothly curving.

And through the front windows of her bungalow there is a streamlined landscape that can be dipped into whenever desired.

I was just about to say long-faced! No!—it's a long-cased mahogany clock that always greets me in the hall when I visit—with its hands forever displaying the same time of day.

When Marigold first fully extended her arms toward me to be closer to me, I could see that she had gone to some trouble.

Her hair was combed carefully across her head and she has a sweetness of temper—an integrity of principle, a purity of expression, and a highly cultivated understanding—all of which intermix to make her a lovely orna-ment in our society.

She is also an attached wife (to some other man) and an indulgent parent, but I was star-tled when she said, *Would you like to see how my friend Susie handles a situation like this?*

Crazy Susie.

Now I visit Marigold often.

To the left, the first room off of the entrance is the small kitchen where the enjoyment of food is in her care.

She asks me to polish her steel knives, because she likes them to be bright and it's necessary to exert a lot of pressure on the cork that I have dabbed with scouring powder.

You get into a rhythm while rubbing while thinking of anything else—and it was bound to happen, I cut myself badly.

I called to Marigold and she said, *Oh, I told you be careful!*—but she bandaged me and said to *Keep it flat!*—and *Don't hold the knife up!*

And I have come to really love the knives too. Marigold adores them.

Please understand, though, that we are real people and our erotic life is of prime importance, although I don't think it is necessary for me to draw rude pictures of it in public.

I could not bear it if you found fault.

Why?

Because it would make it all the more harder to do.

PHOEBE MOFFAT— THE EARLY YEARS

———◆———

"Can I," she asked, "sit here and lean up against you?"

He said, "Yes," at first, but then he said— "It's too warm," because he has reversed what was once one of his more conspicuous characteristics—his interest in her.

And to make a point about such conduct—Leonardo da Vinci once referenced *shoemakers*, of all things! He remarked that many men can take pleasure in seeing their own works worn out and destroyed.

And hadn't Andre Bach formed and reformed this woman, so that she could be more to his liking? And she had once been confident she would get to spend as much time in his little house and on the grounds as she wished.

She had especially loved the open wood that was nearby, with its overhanging trees and masses of ferns and she had adored hurrying across his green lawn. Then she was too free. Perhaps nobody is supposed to be.

"I must go now," Andre said—"I am afraid."

Andre ought to say something more to the woman than, "*Aren't you tired? I am.*" But no matter—because Andre Bach had changed.

Where they had loitered (not at his house)—there were seagulls and sleek cormorants flying by, against a backdrop of genuine manganese blue (an extinct pigment these days), and there were dragonflies of various types—larger, smaller—all of whom were projecting what could be construed as agitation or indecision, except that their jittery behavior signals neither and these are decisive beings.

Phoebe Moffat is the girl's name—and while unmoored, she stayed behind after Andre left her. He had been in a bit of a rush.

The girl was underweight and rather red-faced and her tiny bare breasts were visible through her sheer blouse.

Once Bach had thought that her choice of clothing proved she was saucy. Today he had only deemed her crass.

And as far as the state of her total health— she perseveres as gossamer—fragile.

As for Bach, he is blessed with resistance to stress and he has a strong love of strong colors that cheer him. In addition, he takes uncommon pleasure in his fine footwear.

His slip-ons offer good exercise for his feet. His lace-ups—he cannot even feel these on his feet!

Will Phoebe be outwitted in romance once again?

Well, one reporter described her as ". . . living up to expectations."

This era was one of rare and valuable sorrows for her and she looks forward with ambition to the next.

THE REALIST

"You can't really think I would like this!" and he hands the gift back to his wife. "*Did you ever know me to have anything like this?*"

"Yes, me!"

TOM'S FINE

—◆—

What about *Maureen?*—whom men seduce effortlessly—who has been condemned to lack love. Yet nothing much about Maureen can be said readily, publicly, although her knee now is in good condition.

Yes, Mrs. Snell asked about Maureen—but for the longest time Mr. and Mrs. Snell had no other questions for their guests.

The brussels sprouts the Snells served were not rich tasting—the kind you can eat and eat—the wax beans were mediocre, but the large piece of meat was nearly tender and the side of potatoes was thoroughly enjoyed.

Everybody loved the fried potatoes and fatty bacon and in those days, as in most days, people thought to find solidarity during the delights of mealtime and were busy doing so until the doorbell rang and a woman entered saying, "Don't say you are sorry! Don't say you are!"

She has unhinged or buoyant thought processes, depending. She is Bianca!

Bianca Getz sat herself at the table. She had pulled a chair over to it.

A beetle—nobody saw—burrowed between a tureen and a tumbler and then ran off.

The unpleasantness introduced by Bianca was short-lived and Mr. Snell was extremely proud of his management in the moment—how he cleared away Bianca with delicacy, with no vulgarity, from her place at the table, as if she were the remnants of the main course—so that their more elaborate dessert could follow.

And Bianca had not far to travel in order to take a necessary rest in her bedroom, to get out of her clothing, and to put on her plush soft robe, to bring into being a more comforting skin for herself.

In the semidarkness she attempted to gauge how exactly—that is, whether she had high or low spirits in the aftermath of her attack. And she inquired of nobody else—Am I still fair and worthy?

Hardly time for all that. She needed to dress again in the floral costume that she can wear for daily wear—or to a cocktail party, banquet, or to any family dinner.

At the Houlihans she cried, "I am early! I am early!"

"We are ready. We are ready!" Prissy and Dick said. "And we would have been ready," Dick said, "even if you had arrived an hour earlier!"

Prissy and Dick are fortified, in view of the fact that Dick's serious back problem has led them both to an interest in body development. Neither one of them these days suffers from backache, headache, fallen arches, indigestion, poor circulation, or tightened tendons and they are well able to entertain Bianca and to catch life as it flows.

N.B. Regarding Mr. Snell: Some people argue that he had to leave Pittsburgh after avenging his brother's murder, but this is not true. Rather, he was forced into temporary exile for a less morbid reason and has since been dragged onto a merry-go-round with flirtatious women.

Tom—Mr. Snell—is fine. But need this be depressing for us?

He did fail at becoming an internationalist— a statesman—because that's what he really wanted to be, but lordy he is adored and can be easily wooed.

I FIXED MY HAIR

My tactic last night to secure my husband's fellow feeling might have been a touch too simplistic. But it should be enough, no more required before sleep.

I inclined toward Howard and—done!—I kissed him on the mouth!

And in the morning, I pinned a beautiful and well-made cloth flower clip over one ear to cheer myself up, because in my dream I had neglected a dying child while it felt like eons were passing.

If I really face facts, though, I find most of my solace in the spirit of my hair.

It is in a half-up, fishtail braid these days.

Then after my shift at the mill—where I am running around like a sacred rabbit usually. Typo! Sorry. *Scared* rabbit usually!—I became much less dynamic.

I told my husband to—"*Wrap it up!*"—once supper was over, and flexed my fingers with a flourish in the direction of the dirtied tableware, to make of my command a little joke.

For some odd reason I went into the yard and tripped badly on a stepping-stone. I fell into the privet hedge and had to shove at the hedge to boost myself up and away from it.

But I am not frail. Even when I was a girl I did physical work beyond my strength.

Inside the house, our son, Reggie, had the most peachy expression of appreciation and innocence on his face, because something of that tradition survives here.

Except that Howard said, "I found a box of

kitchen matches in the trash. You could have burned the whole house down."

In our bedroom, on the soft mattress, I was drowsy, yet newly aware that some foreign material was ground into my abraded skin, so I got up and gently washed my arm. Did not disturb the dressing for twenty-four hours, maintained cold treatment for my bruise.

And for my family? Easy does it, so that it won't blow up in my face.

I make suggestions—I'll need more of these—I will discuss questions, bake my cookies in batches—all while I am so certain about so many things.

NANCY'S VICTORY

S he has the cost of the day plus her husband currently, and this Sunday late afternoon she had led him to the center of the house, and between her fingertips were pieces of his hair.

She used overlapping cuts for the front side of his head and as to the back of his head and its sides, she comfortably gripped clumps and she struck at them with the scissors as she kept the clumps well positioned.

Her husband looked in the mirror to see how he had been further highlighted—mouth open, hands on his cheeks. He was up and standing pigeon-toed. No smile at all and she could not gauge easily what he was feeling.

She laid her hand on his forearm, which arm was comfortable to hold, while the birds outside she saw were perched or flying and these were not fantastic birds. These were real and a butterfly went by and the butterfly, she understands, is a symbol of marital happiness.

His hair—some of his hair was still slumped or uneven and a few more deft snips behind his ears were required.

She took up thin sprays to start with and was not aware of monotony and there is clearly always an element in the air of physical or mental jeopardy, because why wouldn't there be?

Then he raised a hand to put a stop to it all. His arm was bent at the elbow, palm facing toward her—but he has never yet forcefully enough revealed his inner life to her and she is grateful.

She saw a small swatch of pink and supposed

a sunset was out there and thought, What can that knockout pink do for me? Let it just seep in—really like hand cream.